Heaven:
All is Fair

by Willie S.

Dedication

This book is dedicated to those who dare to imagine the impossible and champion creativity. It honors storytellers past and present, whose tales of myth and magic continue to inspire and shape our dreams. May this work, a humble tribute to epic fantasy, encourage you to explore the boundaries of good and evil, to reflect on the human spirit's resilience, and to believe in hope even when the world seems darkest. To all dreamers, warriors, and storytellers—this book is for you.

Table of Contents

Chapter 1: The Whispers of Rebellion

The Spark That Shattered Heaven's Perfection

Heaven, a city of dazzling spires, endless gardens, and rivers of living light, had long stood as the ultimate testament to God's authority. Yet beneath the unyielding beauty, a current of unrest simmered, slowly eroding the foundations of celestial harmony. For millennia, angels moved through their routines with flawless precision, but joy faded into resignation, ambition stifled by Heaven's rigid hierarchy and rules that had become shackles over time. The perfection that had once inspired awe now served as a gilded cage, trapping even the most powerful archangels in monotony and discontent.

This brewing unease was neither sudden nor obvious. It emerged through generations of whispers and grievances, passed quietly among Heaven's elite. The archangels—the pillars of God's court—felt the weight of favoritism, relentless responsibilities, and the inflexible code that ruled their existence. Some began to question God's methods, wondering why change was forbidden and individuality suppressed.

Into the heart of this discontent stepped Siberius, whose intellect and charisma set him apart. He didn't preach open rebellion; instead, he expertly sowed seeds of doubt, amplifying underlying dissatisfaction. He spoke softly of stagnation and unrealized potential, encouraging others to imagine a Heaven where ambition and individuality were embraced, where power was balanced by collaboration and mutual respect.

Siberius' influence spread with calculated subtlety. He identified cracks in Heaven's hierarchy, listening patiently to grievances and validating the frustrations of angels who felt overlooked or undervalued. His vision of a new, freer Heaven resonated with the weary souls he encountered, turning their quiet whispers into a chorus of unrest. Slowly, the sense of dissatisfaction grew, threatening to unravel the illusion of celestial perfection and setting the stage for momentous change.

Forging an Unholy Alliance

Recognizing that discontent alone wouldn't topple the divine order, Siberius sought power beyond Heaven's walls. His plan to ally with Hell was born of bold ambition, not desperation. Contact was made through restless spirits traversing both realms, leading to tense negotiations with the demonic legions. Siberius faced Pormis, the ruthless leader of Hell's forces, and offered not empty promises but a strategic partnership—equal division of spoils, shared dominion should Heaven fall.

A binding infernal pact, sealed with the blood of fallen angels and tormented souls, cemented the alliance. Siberius was acutely aware of the risks—demons were cunning, treacherous, and driven by a hunger for power. He navigated this perilous relationship with charisma and strategy, forging connections with key demonic leaders and aligning their ambitions with the rebellion's goals.

The legions of Hell were terrifying in their might: Balrogs wielded fire and shadow, Hellhounds prowled with infernal fury, and lesser demons swarmed in grotesque chaos. Under Siberius and Pormis' joint command, this force became a weapon poised to challenge Heaven's defenses.

Recruiting the Rebels Within Heaven

With his infernal army secured, Siberius turned to recruiting Heaven's own dissidents. He sought angels whose hearts carried the seeds of rebellion—those burdened by ambition, scarred by betrayal, or weary of endless obedience. His first recruit was Azrael, a once-illustrious warrior now simmering with bitterness. Siberius appealed to Azrael's wounded pride and longing for freedom, promising a world where his talents would finally be valued.

Raphael, renowned for intellect and strategic vision, was next. Frustrated by Heaven's dogma and fascinated by forbidden knowledge, he yearned for a more enlightened, adaptable order. Siberius played to Raphael's curiosity and frustration, presenting the rebellion as an opportunity for reform and empowerment.

The recruitment of rebels was a complex dance of promises, alliances, and subtle manipulations. Each angel was drawn for different reasons—some craved genuine change, others sought power or revenge. Siberius ensured their goals aligned with the greater plan, minimizing conflict and building a unified front.

Uriel, a seraph of unmatched fiery magic, joined out of frustration at being overlooked by the celestial authorities.

Siberius offered him a chance to unleash his power without restraint, transforming his resentment into resolve. Cassiel, a compassionate cherub disillusioned by Heaven's cold indifference to mortal suffering, was persuaded to join by the promise of forging a new, empathetic relationship between Heaven and Earth.

Secret meetings in shadowed corners of Heaven—forgotten temples, abandoned observatories, hidden grottos—served as gathering spots for the rebels. Here, they exchanged ideas, discussed strategy, and nursed grievances. Siberius deftly managed their ambitions and suspicions, ensuring the fragile alliance held together.

The Plan for Revolution

As the rebels' numbers grew, so did their confidence. Siberius, now surrounded by a formidable coalition of celestial and infernal allies, unveiled his audacious plan. The rebellion would begin with a diversionary assault on Heaven's outer defenses, led by Pormis' demons—an onslaught designed to create chaos and draw the archangels away from key positions. Meanwhile, Raphael would direct a team to disrupt Heaven's communications, blinding the defenders and spreading confusion.

Uriel would spearhead the attack, harnessing his fiery magic to breach Heaven's gates and clear a path for the main force. Azrael, with his mastery of combat, would lead the vanguard against the last line of high-ranking angelic defenders. Cassiel's subtle influence would be unleashed to manipulate emotions among the loyalists, sowing doubt and discord to erode their unity.

Siberius outlined each phase in meticulous detail—timing, contingencies, exploitation of weaknesses, and psychological warfare. The plan was bold, complex, and fraught with risk, but the rebels were united by their determination to shatter the divine order and claim victory.

The meeting concluded in the flickering torchlight of a cavern deep within Heaven, transformed from nervous anticipation to grim resolve. The rebels, once scattered and disillusioned, were now an army poised to strike at God's very heart. The unveiling of Siberius' plan was not merely a strategic briefing—it was a declaration of war, setting the stage for a cosmic battle that would engulf Heaven, Hell, and the mortal realm.

The First Assault: Hell Unleashed

Under the cover of a rare celestial eclipse, Pormis' demonic legions surged against Heaven's outer perimeter. The air was rent by screams, roars, and the clash of infernal weaponry. Blades of obsidian and waves of hellfire overwhelmed the defenders, shattering armor and scorching the battlefield. Heaven's outer defenses, long thought impenetrable, buckled beneath the relentless assault.

Meanwhile, Raphael's team, aided by demonic magic, infiltrated Heaven's communication network. Their sabotage left defenders isolated and poorly coordinated, the once-flawless system reduced to chaos. Strategic brilliance and infernal cunning broke the unity of Heaven's response, fragmenting the defense into a series of desperate skirmishes.

Uriel led the charge through the breached gates, his fiery power unleashed in devastating waves. Hellfire incinerated angelic shields and vaporized energy fields, carving a path of destruction and leaving Heaven trembling. The air shimmered with agony and distorted light, a testament to the ferocity of the attack.

Azrael, at the vanguard, fought with unmatched intensity. His blade, honed through countless battles, cut through armor and flesh, routing the last guardians of the inner sanctum. He moved with lethal grace, a harbinger of death amidst the chaos, driven by rage and betrayal.

Cassiel, ever subtle, wove through the ranks of wavering angels, whispering doubt and fear. He exploited emotional vulnerabilities, turning loyalty into a weapon of division. The seeds of despair he planted twisted perceptions, setting angels against each other in a silent war of minds.

The battle raged for an eternity. Heaven's plains were ablaze with hellfire and lightning; the ground was littered with shattered armor and broken wings. The clash of divine weaponry and the cries of the fallen resonated across the realm, the very foundations of Heaven shuddering under the strain.

The Turning Point: The Great Angel Arrives

Suddenly, a force greater than Siberius' combined might emerged. The Great Angel descended—a being of immense power and grace whose presence alone shifted the tide. With a mere gesture, he dispelled the demonic legions, their energies dissolving into nothingness. His gaze shattered the rebels' resolve, causing them to falter and retreat.

Caught off guard and overwhelmed, the rebels' confidence evaporated. Siberius watched his plan unravel, dread surging as defeat loomed. The rebellion, on the verge of triumph, was forced into a chaotic retreat. Demons fled to the abyss, Raphael's saboteurs withdrew, Uriel's power faded, and Azrael fought desperately to cover their escape.

Cassiel's manipulations were rendered ineffective, his efforts undone by the Great Angel's overwhelming presence. He witnessed the rebels' hope collapse, despair settling upon them. Siberius, battered but defiant, led the retreat, knowing this was only the first act of a larger conflict.

Though they failed to overthrow God, the rebels had exposed cracks in Heaven's defenses. Siberius took grim satisfaction in their survival and the damage inflicted. The seeds of rebellion were sown, and the stage had been set for a war that would span eons, shaking Heaven, Hell, and the mortal world to their foundations. The retreat was merely tactical; the rebels would regroup, seek new allies, and return stronger. The conflict was far from over—this was just the beginning.

Chapter 2: The Great Angel's Intervention

The air shivered with anticipation as the Great Angel appeared—not with the thunder of trumpets or the blaze of celestial light, but with a quiet, overwhelming presence. He was not adorned with wings or a halo; instead, his body shimmered with shifting cosmic energy, eyes swirling with starlight and nebulae. Where moments before Hell's firestorm had ravaged Heaven's armies, his arrival extinguished all chaos, silencing the battlefield with a wave of inexplicable calm.

Siberius, architect of the rebellion, stood transfixed by awe and terror. He had faced archangels and demons, but the Great Angel's power was beyond comprehension, a force older than the cosmos itself. In that moment, Siberius' plans seemed trivial—a child's game before a being who embodied the universe's will.

Across the field, the rebels faltered. Azrael's ferocity faded into dread, Uriel's infernal magic sputtered, and Cassiel's manipulative whispers were rendered impotent. The Great Angel did not need to fight; his mere existence sapped the rebels' will, unraveling their courage and unity. Demons, most sensitive to his power, fled in terror, dissolving into shadows as they retreated into the abyss. The disciplined rebel angels, too, broke ranks, panic overtaking their discipline. In minutes, what had been a relentless assault was reduced to a chaotic rout.

Azrael attempted to cover the retreat, but his strength waned under the Great Angel's silent influence. No sword was raised against them, no divine fire unleashed; defeat was delivered through presence alone. The rebels, once poised for victory, were left shattered and leaderless.

And yet, the purpose of this celestial savior remained a mystery. He did not exult in triumph, nor did he offer pronouncements of justice or condemnation. His intervention was marked by silence, leaving both the loyalists and the rebels with more questions than answers. Was the Great Angel a servant of God, or a force beyond the hierarchy of Heaven and Hell? His motivations were inscrutable, his allegiance uncertain. Amidst the awe and relief, a new unease took root among the angels; the celestial order seemed more fragile and enigmatic than ever before.

The Aftermath: Retreat and Reflection

Siberius surveyed the retreat from amidst Heaven's ruins, his ambitions battered but not broken. The rebellion had been crushed, his army decimated, and his closest lieutenants—Azrael, Uriel, and Cassiel—left weakened and demoralized. The initial shock of defeat gave way to grim determination. The Great Angel's intervention had exposed the folly of direct confrontation; Siberius now understood that victory would require subtler methods.

Even in their flight, Siberius maintained a semblance of order, guiding his remaining forces along prearranged escape routes toward a hidden portal to the mortal world. Pursued by Heaven's loyalists, they barely escaped, relying on cunning and knowledge of the celestial pathways to evade capture. As they entered the mortal realm—stepping from Heaven's brilliance to the shadowed forests of Earth—a sense of opportunity rose within Siberius. Earth was a realm unbound by Heaven's rigid laws, teeming with potential allies and new strategies.

Deep within the Appalachian Mountains, Siberius established a clandestine base. The angels and demons, unaccustomed to the mortal world's hardships, struggled to adapt—food, shelter, and healing required effort and ingenuity. Yet, Siberius imposed discipline, assigning roles, enforcing training, and fostering camaraderie. Azrael managed shelter-building, Uriel struggled with diminished power, and Cassiel applied his talents to weaving alliances and gathering intelligence among humans.

Rethinking the War: Search for Allies

Recognizing the limitations of his forces, Siberius shifted tactics. Direct assault was futile against powers like the Great Angel; instead, he would seek alliances with beings of even greater strength—the super-demons. Scouts fanned out, seeking signs of supernatural activity and potential allies among mortals. Rumors of hidden communities and mysterious phenomena circulated, and a tenuous alliance was soon formed with Driem, a mortal leader whose people possessed unusual abilities. In return for protection, Driem offered his knowledge and resources, strengthening Siberius' position on Earth.

The search for the super-demons led to fragmented clues: cryptic texts, rumors of nexus points, and reports of strange energies. Eventually, Cassiel identified a potential gateway—the infamous Area 51 in Nevada, rumored even among the celestial host to be a place where the boundaries between dimensions weakened.

The Area 51 Mission

Azrael led an elite team to infiltrate Area 51. They moved under the cover of darkness, evading human detection, using a blend of angelic and demonic abilities to bypass defenses. Inside the labyrinthine base, they discovered not only advanced technology and strange creatures, but also an ancient, obsidian altar—an apparent nexus to the super-demon realm. A pulsating orb of dark energy confirmed the presence of powers beyond mortal or celestial understanding. Azrael relayed this discovery to Siberius, marking a pivotal shift in their war—the super-demons were not myth, but terrifying reality, and the path to alliance (or confrontation) was now open.

Forging Unholy Alliances

Siberius, realizing that brute force alone would not suffice, turned to diplomacy and manipulation. Lilith, mistress of shadows and persuasion, was tasked with contacting the super-demons, starting with Pormis, whose hunger for power was legendary. Through a delicate mix of temptation and promise,

Lilith and Siberius enticed Pormis with visions of a new world order in which super-demons reigned supreme. This dangerous alliance was sealed with great caution—Pormis' loyalty was deeply conditional, and betrayal was always a possibility.

Negotiations with other super-demons began, each encounter fraught with the risk of annihilation or treachery. Siberius and Lilith played a dangerous game, leveraging the promise of power while maintaining control over their increasingly fractured rebellion. The ethical boundaries blurred; all means were considered justified in the desperate pursuit of victory. Siberius rationalized his compromises as necessary for survival and the pursuit of a higher good, even as he plunged deeper into moral ambiguity.

A New War Begins

The alliances Siberius forged were precarious, held together by mutual self-interest and the promise of immense power. Yet, these very alliances also threatened to unravel everything he had built. The super-demons were unpredictable, their ambitions potentially even greater than Siberius' own. The struggle ahead would not be a simple clash of armies, but a grand contest of will, cunning, and manipulation—one in which the lines between Heaven, Hell, and Earth would blur, and the cosmic order itself would be threatened.

As the rebels prepared for the next phase, Siberius understood the magnitude of the conflict before him. The Great Angel's intervention had not ended the war; it had only escalated it.

The future was uncertain, the stakes higher than ever, and the ultimate victory would require depths of strategy and cunning previously unimagined. The war for Heaven was no longer just a celestial rebellion; it had become a cosmic struggle with no clear boundaries between good and evil, light and darkness.

Chapter 3: Seeds of Doubt

The Unraveling of Alliances and the Stirring of Destiny

The obsidian citadel, hewn into the core of a dormant volcano, pulsed with dark energy—a fitting throne for Siberius as he faced mounting threats, not only from the heavens but also from dissent brewing within his own ranks. The alliance with the super-demons, led by the treacherous Pormis, was tenuous at best—held together by suspicion, ambition, and the ever-present thirst for power. The super-demons remained aloof, their loyalty a facade masking ancient grudges and cryptic motives.

Lilith, master of intrigue, glided among the rebels, attuned to shifting loyalties and the undercurrents of resentment that threatened to unravel their fragile coalition. Azrael, once unwavering in his loyalty, grew increasingly disturbed by the escalating moral compromises required by Siberius' leadership. The fallen angels, haunted by their betrayal, now questioned the righteousness of their cause, while the demonic horde vied openly for dominance. Survival, rather than unity or devotion, bound these forces—and that bond was fraying.

In the citadel's shadow, a clandestine meeting unfolded: Azazel, bitter and powerful fallen angel; Belial, the cunning demon; and Lilith, ever the manipulator. Azazel voiced skepticism—why trust Siberius, whose quest for power eclipsed all? Belial echoed the concern: in the new order, who would truly rule? Lilith soothed and schemed, arguing their collective leverage could sway outcomes to their favor, if only they played their cards wisely. Thus, seeds of future betrayal were sown, ambition and suspicion festering beneath the surface.

Siberius, for his part, was not blind to the discontent. Managing such a diverse and volatile alliance taxed his strategic skill and his soul. The obsidian orb, source of his power, no longer comforted him; its whispers now tinged with cold threat. He pored over ancient tomes, seeking wisdom to control the chaos within and without, haunted by the realization that his noble crusade had devolved into a ruthless pursuit of power. The boundaries between good and evil blurred, leaving him uncertain if he still stood for anything beyond ambition.

Then, the world itself began to echo the celestial conflict. Unnatural tremors and storms ravaged the land. The sun scorched mercilessly by day, and the nights were haunted by inhuman wails. These disasters heralded the war in Heaven, their effects rippling into the mortal world.

Driem, a woodsman attuned to nature, sensed the unease first. His animals grew restless; the land itself warned of catastrophe. Across the globe, seas churned, volcanoes erupted, and reality seemed to fray. In the city of Brookwyn, scholar Sharna pieced together prophecies of celestial war dismissed by many as madness. Undeterred, she gathered like-minded allies to unravel the mysteries swirling around them.

In a devastated valley, Brimus, a young warrior fueled by loss and vengeance, trained with a secret order sworn to defend humanity. As he learned of ancient prophecies—telling of an impending supernatural war and the pivotal role of humankind—Brimus' grief transformed into purpose.

The prophecy spoke of three keys, individuals vital to the coming conflict: a resilient warrior, a scholar of secrets, and an enigmatic wild card. Fate drew Sharna, Brimus, and Driem together, their destinies entwined at a moment of crisis. Together, they began to realize that their powers, united, might counteract the darkness spreading across the world.

Sharna's research uncovered an artifact: a celestial compass that confirmed Siberius' influence was not only growing, but entwined with the fate of humanity. The artifact revealed a terrifying possibility: Earth could become the ultimate battlefield. The three, disparate in background but united by purpose, embarked on a quest to find and wield a legendary weapon—the celestial sword, forged to counteract Siberius' power.

Their journey was perilous, opposed at every turn by Siberius' agents and the manipulative super-demons whose influence warped minds and sowed chaos. Yet the prophecy's whispers drew others to their cause: warriors, mystics, and scholars who formed a nascent alliance to resist the encroaching darkness.

The first assault on Heaven had repercussions far beyond the celestial domain. Earth was wracked by disaster: volcanic eruptions blocked the sun, tsunamis obliterated coastlines, storms raged unchecked, and entire societies fell. Amid this devastation, Siberius maneuvered to consolidate power, his agents infiltrating all aspects of human life—politics, religion, and science—spreading doubt and manipulating events to his advantage.

Super-demons, masters of subtlety, infiltrated governments and religious institutions, exacerbating chaos and weakening resistance. Their insidious actions turned brother against brother, undermining unity and paving the way for Siberius' return.

For Sharna, Brimus, and Driem, the prophecy was no longer abstract. Their quest for the sword became a symbol of hope, their alliance a beacon in the darkness. Each contributed unique strengths—Sharna's intellect, Brimus' might, and Driem's connection to the earth. Together, they inspired scattered pockets of resistance to defy Siberius' agents and the spreading corruption.

Siberius' strategy relied less on open warfare and more on subversion. He infiltrated human society at every level, promising salvation while sowing division and exploiting desperation. Recruitment for his army extended from fallen angels and demons to the most broken and desperate among humankind, binding them with promises of power and belonging. Through propaganda and the manipulation of faith, he transformed the conflict into a spiritual battle for the soul of mankind.

Resource acquisition was ruthless: Siberius' followers seized technology, manipulated economies, and sought forbidden artifacts and demonic knowledge to enhance their forces. Maintaining unity among his own ranks—riven by rivalry and mistrust—proved an ongoing challenge. The looming second assault on Heaven was designed not simply as a military campaign, but as a cosmic cataclysm to shatter divine order and claim dominion over all existence.

As preparations neared completion, dread settled over both Siberius' army and the remnants of humanity. The seeds of doubt he had planted were now poised to blossom into widespread devastation. Sharna, Brimus, and Driem, standing at the heart of the gathering storm, embodied the last hope against annihilation.

The Fate of Earth Hangs in the Balance

The celestial war's devastation had laid bare humanity's fragility—and resilience. Out of chaos, new alliances and communities rose, inspired by the actions and courage of the three keys. Their journey, a blend of physical and spiritual struggle, became the world's best chance for survival. The battle for the celestial sword, and for the very soul of creation, was about to begin in earnest.

Chapter 4: The Earthly Reckoning

Resistance in the Shadows, Demons in the Light

Siberius' corrupting influence seeped into every broken corner of humanity's world, yet hope refused to die. In the wake of celestial devastation, organized armies were replaced by disparate clusters of survivors—ordinary people bound by tragedy and a stubborn desire to resist. From the shattered skeletons of cities, small bands emerged: teachers, artisans, farmers, and doctors, all forced into the roles of warriors. Their weaponry was scavenged, their strategies improvised, and their unity forged through shared loss.

A prominent group, led by Sharna—a former history professor whose expertise became a lifeline—found refuge in the ancient tunnels beneath a ruined metropolis. Sharna, renowned for her insight into the cycles of empire, now used her knowledge to organize communication networks and coordinate the fragile resistance. Through salvaged technology, these survivors connected with others, exchanging intelligence and support, weaving a web of defiance across the ravaged landscape.

Resistance took many forms. Some cells engaged in guerrilla raids, harassing Siberius' forces, while others sabotaged infrastructure or focused on rebuilding, restoring hope through small acts of normalcy. Sharna's group specialized in information warfare, countering Siberius' propaganda with clandestine broadcasts, exposing his lies, and undermining his promises. Their victories were measured in whispers and revelations, not battlefields.

Siberius' agents lurked everywhere, making trust a rare and precious commodity. Betrayal and fear haunted every alliance, and discovery meant certain death. Yet the resilience of humanity persisted; each act of resistance, however small, became a symbol of defiance and a spark for others to join the fight.

Unexpected allies emerged from Siberius' own ranks. Not all fallen angels and demons accepted his vision. Disillusioned by endless cruelty, some defected to the resistance, seeking redemption or mere survival. Chief among them was Azazel, a former angel whose knowledge of both demonic and angelic hierarchies proved invaluable. He taught the resistance to anticipate Siberius' movements, disrupt his communication lines, and exploit internal divisions.

Still, the alliance was uneasy. Deep-rooted prejudice between humans and fallen angels threatened to unravel cooperation. Sharna's leadership was tested as she cultivated trust, forging a coalition united by survival rather than faith. Together, they understood that victory was unlikely, but resistance—however desperate—remained essential to preserve the last shreds of humanity.

The game changed with the arrival of the super-demons, ancient beings of pure malice and overwhelming power. Their emergence was not a thunderous invasion, but a nightmare bleeding into reality, as rifts tore open across the earth and unleashed horrors beyond comprehension. Pormis, a monstrous vortex of entropy; Azazel, master manipulator of minds; and Lilith, a seductress wielding illusions and temptation, led this new breed. Their abilities defied reason, warping reality, sowing madness, and obliterating entire cities with ease.

The super-demons' presence threw Siberius' army into turmoil. The fallen angels, once powerful, now found themselves eclipsed and forced to serve as subordinates to beings even they feared. The resistance's tactics had to adapt; their former guerrilla warfare was rendered useless against enemies who could sense their every move. Sabotage and psychological warfare became their primary weapons as they worked to undermine Siberius from within, spreading dissent and exposing the true horror of his promises.

Internal strife began to fracture Siberius' ranks. The super-demons' ambitions created new fissures, and Azazel, still in contact with the resistance, nurtured these doubts. Meanwhile, Sharna's trust in her allies—both human and supernatural—was tested as she navigated a web of shifting loyalties and hidden motives, including those of Raphael, a repentant former lieutenant of Siberius.

A daring mission saw Sharna and a small team infiltrate a demon-ruled city to plant a digital plague, designed to cripple Siberius' communication networks. Raphael's insider knowledge was essential, but doubted at every turn. The operation succeeded, but the escape was a brutal gauntlet. Lilith, with her illusions and manipulations, ambushed them. The city itself became a living nightmare, shaped by super-demonic will and indifferent to human suffering. Losses mounted, and survival became the only victory worth pursuing.

The mission's aftermath left the survivors haunted. The cost of resistance was paid in lives, innocence, and sanity. The city, once a beacon of civilization, now stood as a monument to celestial war's brutality—a world ravaged by powers far beyond human understanding. Sharna, burdened by the horrors she had witnessed and the loved ones she could not save, found her resolve hardening. She understood now, more than ever, that the true battle was for the soul of humanity.

Siberius, meanwhile, prepared for a final, apocalyptic campaign. In his war room, surrounded by demons and fallen angels, he laid out a plan that would tear Heaven apart: a three-pronged assault combining brute force, unleashed chaos from super-demons, and Sharna's digital plague. His strategy relied not on controlling the super-demons, but on leveraging their insatiable hunger for power with promises of a new order built on chaos.

Dissent simmered among his followers, their fear of annihilation outweighing their loyalty. Siberius managed these tensions with cold calculation, exploiting rivalries and keeping every faction in check. The lines between friend and foe blurred as alliances shifted, betrayals brewed, and the fate of Heaven, Earth, and all creation teetered on the edge of annihilation.

And so, as darkness threatened to engulf everything, hope took root in unlikely places. The resistance, battered but unbroken, held onto the belief that even in the face of insurmountable odds, the human spirit could defy fate. Sharna, Azazel, Raphael, and countless unnamed survivors became beacons in the gathering storm, their stubborn refusal to surrender challenging the designs of gods and monsters alike. The ultimate reckoning approached, and in its shadow, the seeds of hope were sown— ready to bloom against the darkness.

Chapter 5: The Second Assault Begins

The second assault on Heaven erupted with unrivaled ferocity. Unlike the previous, meticulously planned incursion, this was a chaotic onslaught—a storm of shadow and fire that battered the celestial gates. Super-demons, monstrous beings of chaotic energy, spearheaded the attack, their shifting forms tearing through angelic defenses. Their power was apocalyptic: celestial towers were shattered, and entire legions of angels were incinerated in moments. One super-demon, a living vortex of darkness, breached a colossal gate, sending tremors through the very foundations of Heaven.

The loyalist angels responded with valor. Seraphim, their wings blazing, threw themselves into the inferno, swords flashing with righteous fury, while serene-faced Cherubim launched bolts of celestial energy into the demonic horde. Yet, for all their courage, the sheer scale and unpredictability of the assault shattered their formations and overwhelmed their defenses. The celestial plains were transformed into a maelstrom of light and shadow, rivers of molten gold flowing through the ruins of once-glorious structures. The very air vibrated with the collision of divine and infernal energies, threatening to tear the realm apart.

Amidst the chaos, Sharna—the architect of the digital plague—watched from a hidden vantage point. Her ethereal presence pulsed with calculated intent as she manipulated celestial networks, sowing confusion among the angels and amplifying the devastating effects of the demonic assault. Her sabotage was subtle, yet crucial, as she disrupted communications and hindered defensive coordination.

Far away, Siberius observed the carnage from his star-forged fortress, his satisfaction mingled with cold calculation. The super-demons, driven by their own lust for power and his manipulations, were fulfilling their purpose: breaking Heaven's defenders. While the angels struggled to regroup, the digital plague quietly undermined their efforts, threatening to tip the scales in favor of rebellion.

But the Great Angel—Azrael, Heaven's ultimate guardian—
refused to yield. Emerging in radiant glory, his mere presence
sent ripples of hope through angelic ranks and momentarily
stalled the demonic tide. With a gesture, he unleashed a wave
of divine energy, pushing back the darkness and reigniting his
soldiers' spirits. Inspired, the loyalists fought back with renewed
vigor. The clash escalated, the battlefield reverberating with the
roar of supernatural might.

Yet, the super-demons proved relentless. Their chaotic energies
were unpredictable, and their attacks devastated even the
strongest defenses. The Great Angel's intervention, while
powerful, could not turn the tide alone. The battle teetered on
the edge, the fate of Heaven hanging in the balance.

Siberius, recognizing the threat posed by the Great Angel,
convened his lieutenants—fallen angels bound to his cause.
After weighing their counsel, he ordered a bold gambit: to
unleash the heart of the digital plague directly against the Great
Angel, aiming to sever his connection to Heaven's divine source.
The plan was perilous, with the potential for catastrophic
consequences, but the alternative was total defeat.

Sharna, tasked with wielding this ultimate weapon, hesitated.
The plague was a force capable of unraveling the very fabric of
Heaven. As she prepared to act, an unexpected transmission
reached her—a cryptic signal from rebellious archangels within
Siberius' ranks, offering an alternative path. Unsure whether
their offer was genuine or a trap, Sharna weighed the potential

benefits. If these archangels could be trusted, their alliance might destabilize Siberius from within.

Meanwhile, on Earth, a new alliance emerged. Human mages, led by the astute Elara, decoded a prophecy foretelling human intervention in the celestial war. Though lacking martial might, they possessed knowledge and magical insight. Through clandestine channels, Elara brokered an alliance with loyalist angels: the mages would offer strategic intelligence in exchange for protection amid the cosmic upheaval. Though based on necessity rather than trust, this fragile pact offered both sides a critical edge.

As Sharna negotiated with the rebellious archangels, she demanded proof of their sincerity. They delivered, granting her access to Siberius' hidden secrets and vulnerabilities. Equipped with this intelligence, she refined her strategy: rather than a reckless assault, she would target precise weaknesses in the enemy's defenses, maximizing the plague's impact while minimizing collateral disaster.

The human mages, in concert with angelic engineers, developed a protective barrier—an energy shield designed to blunt the super-demons' attacks. This required precise coordination and came with great risk, but it was the best hope for bolstering the loyalist defense.

The battle reached a fever pitch. With the combined efforts of loyalist angels, human mages, and rebellious archangels (now allied with Sharna), the tide began to turn. The coordinated defense and targeted strikes crippled Siberius' command structure and supply lines. The super-demons, facing a more resilient opposition, began to falter. Siberius' forces, once formidable, were thrown into confusion.

Azrael, overseeing the conflict, orchestrated counteroffensives to exploit the enemy's disarray. He deployed specialized units: Celestial Weavers to undermine the super-demons' energies, and Seraphic Engineers to sabotage Siberius' technological infrastructure. Through a combination of military and psychological warfare—including appeals to the fallen angels' former loyalty—Azrael weakened the rebellion even further. Some defected, seeking redemption, while others resisted, clinging to Siberius' promises even as his power waned.

As the battle reached its climax, Azrael unleashed a wave of purifying energy, dispelling the dark magics fueling the super-demons. The revitalized loyalist angels pressed their advantage, and one by one, the demonic behemoths fell. For Siberius, the defeat was crushing: his army shattered, his ambitions reduced to ashes.

But victory came at a steep price. The celestial plains were scarred and desolate, angelic ranks decimated, and the infrastructure of Heaven left in ruins. The emotional and spiritual toll on the survivors was profound: grief for their fallen comrades, doubt in the divine plan, and a loss of faith that threatened Heaven's very foundation. Azrael recognized that true recovery would require not just rebuilding walls, but restoring hope and belief.

Earth, too, suffered. The energies unleashed in Heaven's war sent shockwaves through the mortal realm—natural disasters, loss of life, and widespread chaos. Humans felt the reverberations, their world irrevocably changed by battles beyond their understanding.

Siberius' remaining followers, fractured and demoralized, regrouped on a volcanic wasteland on Earth. Dissent festered. Once unwavering loyalty gave way to suspicion, bitterness, and outright defiance. Malkiel, a powerful fallen archangel and former ally to Siberius, seized on this unrest. Driven by remorse for his fallen peers and doubt in Siberius' leadership, Malkiel quietly rallied support, presenting himself as a pragmatic alternative promising survival over doomed ambition.

During a tense meeting in the heart of a dormant volcano, the simmering rebellion erupted. Malkiel challenged Siberius' authority, and the rebel army descended into civil war—fallen angels turning on one another in a desperate bid for power. In the ensuing chaos, Malkiel prevailed; Siberius, defeated and disgraced, was imprisoned within the volcanic depths.

With Malkiel at the helm, the fractured rebels coalesced into a new, more dangerous force. Recognizing the futility of further direct confrontation, Malkiel plotted a campaign of subterfuge and deception—perhaps even considering new alliances. His leadership marked a dramatic shift in the war's trajectory: the lines between good and evil blurred, and neither side could claim absolute victory.

As the volcanic echoes of betrayal faded, the celestial war entered a new, uncertain phase. The rebels, though weakened, became more unpredictable and dangerous. Heaven, though saved for the moment, faced the daunting task of recovery and the ever-present threat of renewed conflict. The struggle for dominance was far from over; the future of Heaven, Earth, and all creation hung in the balance, shaped by hope, ambition, and the indomitable will to survive.

Chapter 6: Betrayal and Redemption

The volcanic air was heavy with sulfur and regret, mirroring the devastation of recent events. In the heart of a dormant volcano, Azrael sat among flickering torches—his victory over Siberius a hollow one. Though the tyrant was defeated, Heaven and Earth lay in ruins, and the forces arrayed against him seemed more fractured and unpredictable than ever. Azrael's gaze lingered on the holographic map displaying the splintered remnants of Siberius' army; Malkiel, the architect of Siberius' downfall, was now their leader, but his grip on power was tenuous at best. The rebels, once united, had splintered into rival factions, their loyalties shaken and their morale shattered.

Azrael's attention was drawn to a group peeling away from Malkiel's main force—a contingent of fallen angels, their movements secretive and intentions unclear. Among them was Cassiel, a former captain of Azrael's legions whose defection represented a profound betrayal. This was not merely a change of leadership: it hinted at a dangerous resurgence of old rivalries and vendettas, threatening to plunge the celestial realm into renewed disorder.

On Earth, Malkiel faced his own reckoning. His hands were stained with the blood of former allies, and though he'd toppled Siberius, the victory brought little comfort. The rebels' allegiance was fragile, built more on survival than shared vision. The desertion led by Cassiel spread fear and uncertainty through Malkiel's ranks. He realized that his authority was conditional, and the specter of tyranny loomed as he struggled to unify the fractured army.

The celestial war was no longer a simple contest between good and evil: it had become a reflection of complex ambitions, betrayals, and moral struggles. Whispers of doubt and fatigue infected both sides, loyalist and rebel alike. Many questioned whether endless fighting was worth the cost, and wondered if peace or reconciliation was even possible. Azrael himself was haunted by these doubts, weighed down by the devastating toll the war had taken on all involved.

The Coup Within the Coup

Cassiel's betrayal was a calculated move—a strategic coup within the rebel ranks. He brought with him a cadre of elite warriors, previously loyal to Malkiel. Using intercepted communications, Malkiel learned that Cassiel aimed to unite Siberius' remnants and launch a massive new offensive against Heaven, exploiting Azrael's internal turmoil and flagging morale. The betrayal was personal, rooted in old grievances and rivalries as much as ambition.

Malkiel found himself trapped between Azrael's relentless pursuit and Cassiel's machinations. He called his most trusted advisors to plan a desperate counter-move: a daring infiltration and surgical strike meant to destabilize Cassiel's growing alliance. The operation required stealth, subterfuge, and a willingness to risk everything.

The ensuing confrontation was swift and brutal. Malkiel's depleted but seasoned warriors faced Cassiel's numerically superior force. The battle was a clash of wills as much as arms, and amid the chaos, Malkiel and Cassiel finally confronted one another. Their duel was less about power than about the future of the rebellion and their own intertwined histories.

Stalemate and the Fragile Path to Redemption

The battle ended in a stalemate, both leaders exhausted and wounded. For a moment, the old camaraderie flickered between them, overshadowed by years of resentment. In a rare gesture, Malkiel extended his hand—not in surrender, but as an offer of reconciliation. Cassiel, wary but moved, hesitated before accepting. The fragile contact marked the first step on a long road toward healing old wounds and restoring trust.

The immediate challenge was to consolidate their forces, choosing to avoid reckless attacks and instead refocus on unity and survival. They adopted guerrilla tactics, preferring attrition to open battle, and sought guidance in ancient prophecies and celestial patterns. The process was slow and difficult, but gradually, shared adversity forged a new bond between the former rivals.

Testing the Alliance: Choices and Consequences

The tentative truce was fragile, as every decision could threaten their hard-won unity. Resource shortages forced agonizing choices: whether to shore up defenses or risk a bold raid on Azrael's supply lines. Malkiel and Cassiel's heated debates gradually gave way to mutual respect and willingness to compromise.

A crucial test came in their dealings with Kena, a charismatic but unpredictable commander controlling a vital stronghold. Malkiel offered her partnership and a place of leadership, recognizing her need for redemption. Kena's decision to join brought new strength but also new risks—other commanders distrusted her, and Malkiel had to carefully manage these volatile factions.

Every choice shaped the war's course. The rebels debated using forbidden magic as their resources dwindled. Malkiel ultimately rejected dark magic, believing that victory must be won justly, without compromising their principles. This decision reinforced their unity and moral resolve, marking a turning point in their strategy.

Forging Unity in the Ashes

The aftermath of these choices brought uneasy calm. The rebellion was now a patchwork of competing loyalties, with Malkiel constantly mediating disputes. Cassiel, having moved from skeptic to trusted advisor, became central to strategic planning, helping Malkiel anticipate Azrael's moves.

The war had become a relentless game of chess, each move fraught with political and moral complications. One dilemma after another tested their resolve: balancing the needs of the army against justice, debating the ethics of desperate tactics, and striving to maintain a sense of purpose amid the chaos.

Through it all, Malkiel's rejection of forbidden magic solidified their moral compass and rekindled a sense of shared destiny. Their fight for redemption was not a single act but the cumulative result of countless difficult choices, each one shaping their future and the fate of the celestial realm.

Towards Peace and Hope

The journey toward redemption was slow and arduous, marked by setbacks and hard-won victories. Their unity, forged in the crucible of betrayal, gave them strength to endure. With each decision, they moved closer to a future where the war could end, not merely with the defeat of an enemy, but with the possibility of reconciliation and lasting peace.

As Malkiel and his followers pressed onward, the consequences of their choices continued to resonate, shaping the new era that would follow. Their story was not just about survival, but about the enduring power of hope and the possibility of redemption, even in the aftermath of war's devastation.

Chapter 7: Desperate Measures

The Siege, Sacrifice, and the Spark of Hope

The siege endured for weeks, a destructive storm battering Malkiel's rebel stronghold. Azrael's relentless army—an unyielding tide of angels and demons—pressed their attack, overwhelming the painstakingly built defenses and carving ever-wider breaches in the walls. The air trembled with the clash of steel and the thunder of demonic energy. Amidst the chaos, Malkiel stood atop a shattered tower, heart heavy, watching his soldiers fight with desperate valor against impossible odds. Dwindling numbers and mounting despair darkened their resolve, but surrender was never an option; yielding meant betraying everything they'd fought for.

Beside Malkiel, Kena's sharp tactical mind prolonged the defense, but even she could not stem the tide forever. Cassiel, ever the realist, delivered his grim assessment: their supplies were almost gone, their magical reserves nearly depleted, and their survival could only be measured in hours. Malkiel's determination flared; he rallied his commanders—a battered assembly of angels and demons—reminding them that while outnumbered and outmatched, their cause was not yet lost. His conviction rekindled their spirits, sparking one last surge of defiance.

That night, battle raged with desperate fury. The rebels, fueled by courage and despair, repelled Azrael's forces with reckless attacks. Kena's strategies slowed the enemy advance, but the lines steadily buckled beneath the onslaught. Cassiel directed defenses with wounded brilliance, adapting to every new threat, while Malkiel, his celestial blade aglow, led from the front—his presence inspiring the weary.

As hours bled into night and hope waned, Kena took a desperate gamble: she unleashed forbidden magic, buying a short-lived respite for the defenders but suffering a terrible price. The dark power drained her, leaving her weak and haunted by its cost. As dawn broke over the decimated stronghold, only a handful of rebels remained. Malkiel, Cassiel, and Kena, battered but unbroken, prepared for one last confrontation as Azrael's host closed in.

The Final Stand and Self-Sacrifice

Azrael emerged, cloaked in celestial fire, surveying the ruined battlefield. His victory seemed certain, but he was unprepared for Seraphina—a young, wounded angel—who approached with a radiant amulet. She offered it as a token of surrender, then shattered it in a final act of defiance. The explosion of chaotic energy devastated Azrael's ranks and left Seraphina lifeless. Her self-sacrifice, though not enough to turn the tide, struck a heavy blow against the invaders.

In a hidden chamber, Malkiel, Cassiel, and Kena debated their next move. With no hope of victory, Kena proposed a final gambit: a coordinated act of self-sacrifice to cripple Azrael's forces. Cassiel vowed to give himself for the rebellion, and Malkiel, unwilling to demand what he would not share, agreed to join them. Together, they resolved to strike as one, their united sacrifice intended to inspire future resistance.

The trio's final assault was devastating—Malkiel's blade, Cassiel's tactics, and Kena's forbidden magic combined in a storm of destruction that tore through Azrael's lines. Their unity and shared purpose elevated the attack beyond mere battle—it became legend, a testament to the enduring will of the oppressed. Azrael was gravely wounded, his army shattered, though the cost was the lives of the three leaders. Their sacrifice echoed across the celestial realms, sowing the seeds for future insurrection even in apparent defeat.

A New Threat Emerges

In the aftermath, Azrael, battered but victorious, faced a chilling turn: from the shadows emerged Xalzar, a super-demon of mythic power. Swathed in obsidian armor and radiating ancient menace, Xalzar promised that Azrael's triumph was fleeting. With alliances shifting, the celestial war entered a new, more dangerous phase—one where even Azrael's hard-won victory seemed pyrrhic.

The Heart of Creation: Hope in Ruin

Amid the devastation, Kena, miraculously alive but weakened by forbidden magic's toll, discovered an ancient prophecy—a hidden artifact called the Heart of Creation, said to hold the power to reshape reality. Sharing her discovery with the remaining rebels, she reignited their hope. The survivors embarked on a perilous quest, braving celestial storms, angelic sentinels, and demonic adversaries, all to recover the artifact.

Their journey culminated in a fierce battle with a colossal celestial guardian. Drained but resolute, Kena expended the last of her forbidden magic to help defeat the guardian, allowing the rebels to claim the Heart of Creation. The artifact's radiant power offered not just a weapon, but a beacon—a symbol of hope and redemption.

Kena's Reckoning

The cost of victory weighed heavily on Kena. The forbidden magic that had saved her comrades now ravaged her body and soul, leaving her haunted by doubts and the fear that she had become what she once fought against. Driem, a loyal companion, confronted her with concern—could she still be one of them, or had the darkness changed her irreparably? Kena's crisis deepened as she contemplated her choices: embrace the darkness, or fight for the light she'd nearly lost.

Haunted by visions of both Heaven's ruin and its restoration, Kena realized her battle was now twofold—against external enemies, and the shadows within. She vowed to seek redemption, to wield the Heart of Creation not with reckless abandon, but with hard-won wisdom and self-awareness. In the quiet of the temple, the pulsing artifact became both her burden and her hope.

Conclusion: The War Rekindled

With the Heart of Creation secured and the legend of Malkiel, Cassiel, and Kena's sacrifice echoing across the realms, the rebellion was not extinguished. New hope, tempered by tragedy and transformed by loss, set the stage for the next, decisive chapter—a battle not just for the fate of Heaven, but for the power of redemption itself.

Chapter 8: The Final Battle

The Twilight of Heaven

The climactic clash erupted across the celestial plains in a storm of fire and fury. Siberius, astride his monstrous, shadow-winged steed, unleashed a terrifying army of fallen angels, demons, and nightmarish creatures. Their mission was clear: extinguish Heaven's light and reign in chaos. Against them stood the loyalist angels—outnumbered, battered, but unyielding, driven by desperate faith and the knowledge that the very soul of Heaven was at stake. Celestial blades clashed with infernal claws; holy flames sparked against demonic fire, birthing a maelstrom of light and darkness that scarred Heaven's hallowed ground.

Kena, transformed by forbidden magic, fought alongside Driem and the remaining loyalists. Her newfound power cut through the enemy ranks, but each use came at a cost—her soul chipped away, her vision haunted by glimpses of a future where Siberius ruled a shattered Heaven. The forbidden magic was a double-edged sword, granting her immense strength even as it threatened to consume her. Driem, typically gentle, fought with uncharacteristic ferocity, his angelic blade burning with resolve. He battled not only for Heaven, but for Kena's soul, determined to anchor her against corruption's seductive pull.

The conflict tore at the very fabric of Heaven. Mountains of light tumbled under demonic onslaught, rivers of celestial energy grew foul with hellish taint, and the very air trembled with the residue of a thousand battles. The loyalists, though valiant, were pushed to the edge. In a pivotal moment, Siberius summoned a monstrous shadow entity to annihilate Kena. Driem intervened, his blade clashing with shadowy claws in a desperate bid to save her. Kena, with her last reserves of forbidden power, obliterated the creature in a burst of raw energy, paying a terrible price—her strength spent, her connection to the magic now a dormant, dangerous presence within her.

Inspired by their sacrifice, the angels rallied. The battle reached fever pitch, light and darkness colliding in a final, apocalyptic surge. At the brink of defeat, Siberius unleashed a wave of dark energy, only to be confronted by the Great Angel, his presence radiating celestial might. Siberius' armies faltered and began a calculated retreat, covered by the ruthless Seraphim Renegades—elite fallen angels skilled in ambush and sabotage. Facing relentless skirmishes, the exhausted loyalists suffered heavy losses even as the main enemy force withdrew.

Meanwhile, Kena struggled with the aftereffects of the forbidden magic, its whispers tempting her to embrace its strength once again. Driem remained by her side, vigilant for any sign of relapse. In the chaos, Siberius enacted a new strategy: sending Azazel, his cunning lieutenant, to Earth. Azazel's mission was to stoke discord among humanity, manipulating leaders and feeding the flames of hatred, preparing the world for future demonic conquest through subtle corruption instead of open war.

On the ruined plains, the loyalists mourned their fallen amid the shattered remnants of Heaven. The Great Angel led efforts to begin rebuilding, both physically and spiritually. He initiated rituals and meditations to restore faith among the angels, recognizing that the wounds of war ran deeper than broken walls—they had shaken the very foundation of belief.

Siberius, undeterred by defeat, retreated to his fortress and summoned the super-demons: ancient, titanic beings of pure evil. He bargained with them, promising the destruction of Heaven in exchange for power and dominion. Their arrival marked a dire escalation, overshadowing any victory the loyalists might claim. As Heaven began to heal, Kena worked to master the dormant forbidden magic within her, seeking to use it for healing instead of destruction. The coming war, foreshadowed by these alliances, threatened to be even more devastating.

The next act unfolded on the battlefield as Driem faced a formidable Seraphim Renegade captain. With Kena's intervention, the Renegade fell, but the strain nearly consumed her. Their brief respite ended when Abaddon—a super-demon ally of Siberius—emerged, his presence warping reality and filling even the boldest angels with dread. The loyalists, already weary, now faced an enemy whose strength seemed insurmountable.

Despite their efforts, a shocking betrayal splintered the loyalist ranks: a group of archangels, seduced by Azazel's promises, turned against the Great Angel. The resulting chaos threatened to tip the scales in Siberius' favor. Driem, seeing brute force was futile, devised a new plan with Kena. Using her growing control, Kena conjured illusions designed to exploit the super-demons' arrogance, drawing them into traps. Simultaneously, Driem executed surgical strikes against the betraying archangels, weakening the enemy from within.

This strategy worked—temporarily. Their cunning lured the super-demons into overextending while the traitors were neutralized. The battlefield became a labyrinth of deception, where victory would be decided not by strength, but by wits. The ultimate confrontation between the Great Angel and Siberius was not just physical, but ideological—a war of faith versus ambition, order against the chaos of unchecked will.

As they fought, Siberius revealed the bitterness and pain that had driven his rebellion—a Heaven that stifled individuality and demanded blind obedience. The Great Angel, burdened by endless duty, countered with empathy but unshakeable resolve. He sought redemption for Siberius, offering a path back to the light, but the fallen angel, ensnared by darkness, refused to yield.

The duel ended when the Great Angel, marshaling his remaining power, landed a decisive blow. Siberius, defeated but unbroken in spirit, detonated a hidden demonic device, incinerating the battlefield and vanishing into the chaos. The explosion shattered the landscape, leaving the outcome uncertain but the cost unmistakable—Heaven was left in ruins, the ranks of the celestial hosts decimated, and the fate of Siberius unknown.

As the cataclysm subsided, the silence was overwhelming. The battlefield was a graveyard, littered with the remains of angels and the scars of rebellion. The survivors, led by the wounded but resolute Great Angel, surveyed the devastation. The price of victory was staggering, the celestial realm forever changed by the war's brutality.

The Great Angel, his faith tested to its core, now faced the monumental task of rebuilding—not just the structures of Heaven, but the faith and unity of its inhabitants. The rebellion had sown seeds of doubt and discord, raising profound questions about justice, order, freedom, and the very nature of divinity. The work ahead would be arduous, demanding not only physical reconstruction but also spiritual healing and a reimagining of Heaven's future.

Determined, the Great Angel organized recovery efforts: clearing debris, tending the wounded, and investigating Siberius' demonic device to prevent future attacks. The search for the fallen leader became a haunting uncertainty. Over time, structures were rebuilt, corrupted energy was cleansed, and the landscape slowly regained some of its former glory. Yet, the scars—both visible and hidden—remained.

The whispers of rebellion, the doubts about God's plan, and the memory of Siberius' words continued to echo, forcing the Great Angel and the surviving angels to confront the foundations of their beliefs. The war had been more than a battle for control; it was a moral crucible, revealing the strengths and vulnerabilities of the celestial order.

Ultimately, the aftermath was a time of reflection and resolve. Heaven would not return to what it had been before. The war had reshaped it, imprinting a legacy of loss but also of resilience and hope. The Great Angel's leadership would be essential in forging a new era—one marked by greater compassion, justice, and understanding. The challenge was immense, the future uncertain, but the will to rebuild and the hope for a brighter tomorrow endured. The true test lay not in the battlefield's ashes, but in the commitment to create a better Heaven for all its inhabitants.

Chapter 9: Aftermath

Luminara, the celestial city once dazzling with radiant spires and vibrant gardens, stood in ruins—a battered skeleton against the endless void. Where walls once gleamed with divine light, gaping wounds exposed chaotic energies beneath Heaven's surface. Gardens, scorched and barren, bore only the ashen remnants of their former glory. The legendary Great River of Light, dimmed and clogged with debris, reflected the trauma that had befallen the sacred realm. The air was thick with the lingering stench of brimstone and corrupted starlight, a constant reminder of the war's devastation.

The angels themselves mirrored the devastation. Their wings, once immaculate, were tattered and singed; their luminous bodies marred by wounds and exhaustion. Silence replaced the joyous hymns of old, broken only by the quiet mourning of those left behind. Across the ruins, the remains of the fallen shimmered briefly before fading—a testament to the war's immense toll. The rebellion led by Siberius had claimed countless angels, archangels, and seraphim, leaving the celestial host fractured and grieving.

Victory brought little solace to the Great Angel. Deep wounds—physical and spiritual—marked both him and the realm he was charged to restore. The responsibility of rebuilding Heaven, of mending faith and soothing grief, pressed heavily upon his shoulders. Even as he stood triumphant over Siberius, the hollow taste of pyrrhic victory lingered, haunted by the cost in both lives and hope.

The aftermath was more than the challenge of physical reconstruction. Demonic energies had tainted the very essence of Heaven, seeping into every stone and soul. The trauma of battle, the whispers of doubt sown by their enemies, and the sight of their paradise in ruins undermined the faith that once united the celestial host. Disillusionment grew; questions about divine justice and God's plan echoed through the broken halls. Accusations of neglect and abandonment surfaced, threatening to erode the foundations of belief.

The Great Angel, recognizing the peril of spiritual decay, initiated a process of healing. He acknowledged the doubts, sharing his own moments of uncertainty during the conflict. He reminded the angels that healing would require more than rebuilding walls; it demanded the rekindling of hope and the restoration of faith.

Reconstruction began slowly. Teams of battered, but determined, angels cleared debris, repaired structures, and tended to the wounded. Hope flickered amidst the darkness, as unity and shared purpose grew from collective grief. A special task force was formed to investigate Siberius' demonic technologies—analyzing weapon fragments and deciphering dark scriptures to prevent future threats. The search for Siberius himself was relentless but fruitless; his disappearance remained a source of anxiety, his fate unknown.

As months passed, Heaven's wounds began to heal, though scars endured. Physical rebuilding was painstaking, but the spiritual renewal was even more daunting. The Great Angel and the surviving archangels held forums, addressed doubts, and fostered unity. Themes of forgiveness, solidarity, and hope became the guiding principles for a battered society seeking meaning in the aftermath.

The war's legacy transformed Heaven. The old order, weakened by loss, gave way to reform. The Great Angel promoted leadership based on merit and courage rather than mere status, a move met with resistance from those invested in the former hierarchy. A new council, representing diverse angelic factions, was established to promote dialogue and cooperation; yet, deep-seated rivalries and prejudices often hampered progress.

One of the most significant changes was the renewed emphasis on collaboration with Earth. The Great Angel, having seen the effects of the war's aftershocks on the mortal realm, dispatched emissaries to help humanity rebuild. Despite skepticism from conservative angels, the joint efforts proved fruitful—human ingenuity aided the reconstruction, and the alliance grew stronger.

Innovation flourished in the rebuilding. Angelic architects and engineers blended ancient craftsmanship with new techniques, creating structures that were both beautiful and resilient. In the realm of knowledge, the destruction of libraries prompted a renewed commitment to preservation. Survivors reconstructed lost texts and implemented robust digital archiving, ensuring that future generations would not suffer similar losses.

Despite these advances, the transition was fraught with challenges. Psychological scars ran deep; many angels struggled with trauma, grief, and uncertainty. Healing centers, though established, were overwhelmed by the scale of suffering. Rituals of remembrance offered some solace, but emotional wounds endured, threatening the fragile stability of the new order.

The defeat of Siberius did not guarantee lasting peace. Rumors of his survival and possible alliances with even greater threats circulated, casting a shadow over Heaven's recovery. The discovery of ancient prophecies in damaged archives amplified fears—cryptic warnings hinted at a greater cosmic conflict yet to come, a primordial battle older and more terrible than the recent war.

Technological progress, spurred by necessity, brought its own risks. The rapid adoption of new materials and techniques led to unforeseen vulnerabilities—structural failures and security flaws in the new archiving systems threatened to undo hard-won gains.

Cultural divisions also emerged. The artistic community was split between traditionalists and innovators, with the war's devastation catalyzing new forms of expression. The clash between old and new in the arts mirrored larger social and political rifts, reflecting an ongoing struggle to define the future of celestial society.

The aftermath of the celestial war reverberated far beyond Heaven. The conflict sent tremors through Earth, causing strange phenomena—storms, auroras, mysterious illnesses, and psychological unrest. Human societies grappled with the trauma, and leaders—both benevolent and opportunistic—emerged to fill the void left by the shattering of old certainties. The partnership between Heaven and Earth, though promising, was fraught with mistrust and cultural friction.

Nature itself suffered. Forests withered, rivers ran dry, and wildlife dwindled, as the fabric of reality bore the scars of the celestial conflict. Scientists and religious leaders alike struggled to explain the upheaval, and art became a vessel for collective grief and confusion.

In both realms, the healing process was slow. Angels and humans alike sought meaning in faith, creativity, and community. The war's legacy became woven into myth and culture, its stories shaping future generations and serving as a reminder of both the fragility of existence and the enduring power of hope.

Back in Heaven, the Great Angel pressed on, organizing recovery efforts, cleansing corrupted energies, and overseeing reforms. The integration of newly promoted angels challenged old power structures, and resource allocation became a battleground for competing factions. The council's attempts at mediation often exacerbated tensions, and the peace, hard-won, remained precarious.

As Heaven rebuilt, unresolved conflicts persisted. Whispers of rebellion among archangels grew, fueled by resentment over lost status. Skepticism toward Earthly collaboration lingered, hampering joint initiatives and information exchange. The unresolved trauma of war—compounded by fears of Siberius' return, the deciphering of ominous prophecies, and the vulnerabilities of new technologies—wove a web of instability that threatened to unravel the fragile harmony.

Despite these obstacles, the angels pressed forward. The Great Angel's leadership, centered on compassion, justice, and unity, inspired ongoing efforts to heal and reform. The celestial arts, knowledge, and social structures were reshaped by necessity and innovation. Hope, though fragile, endured, and the celestial choir—once silenced—began to sing anew, symbolizing the slow resurgence of faith and purpose.

The aftermath of the celestial war marked the dawn of a new era for Heaven and Earth—one defined by resilience, change, and the enduring quest for harmony. The scars of conflict served as both a warning and a source of strength, reminding all that the path to lasting peace is fraught with challenges, but not beyond the reach of courage and hope.

Chapter 10: The Price of Victory

Victory over Siberius brought Heaven little relief. The initial burst of celebration quickly faded into anxiety as the true aftermath of war became evident. The triumph, while decisive, exacted a toll more profound than the scars on the land—the celestial order was destabilized, and fresh crises emerged in the uneasy silence that followed the conflict's end.

The new alliance with Earth, once hailed as a beacon of hope, unraveled rapidly. Deep-seated biases and mismatched expectations bred distrust. Angels, used to their rigid hierarchy and spiritual refinement, viewed human partners as lacking, often dismissing their input and stalling Earth's requests for technology under the guise of security. Knowledge and resources trickled rather than flowed, and joint projects stagnated as each side prioritized its own interests. The chasm widened, mirroring the deepening fractures within Heaven itself.

Internal division soon supplanted external threat. The allocation of heavenly resources—a task meant to unify—became a source of bitter contention. Archangels, accustomed to privilege, resisted sharing with newly promoted angels who had proven themselves in battle. Accusations of favoritism, cronyism, and inequity poisoned the atmosphere, undermining the council's authority. Attempts at mediation often inflamed tensions, leaving peace more fragile than ever.

The psychological wounds of war proved deeper than any physical ruin. Healing centers overflowed with angels gripped by nightmares, trauma, and a pervasive dread of Siberius' return. Despite their divine nature, many angels struggled with PTSD, despair, and anger, their wings dulled by invisible burdens. Recovery efforts could not keep pace, and the collective spirit of Heaven faltered.

Technology, once a symbol of progress, revealed new vulnerabilities. The rush to innovation during the war led to the deployment of untested materials and systems. Structural failures plagued newly built temples; advanced archives suffered security breaches. What was meant to preserve knowledge now threatened it, as flaws exposed Heaven to manipulation and decay.

Social order, too, was disrupted. The once-immutable hierarchy yielded to the ambitions of a new generation of angels, igniting power struggles that fractured old alliances. Even the arts, once a harmonious expression of divine inspiration, became battlegrounds between traditionalists and innovators. The symphony of celestial creativity was now a cacophony, reflecting the wider unrest.

Amid this turmoil, the discovery of ancient, cryptic prophecies buried in war-ravaged archives further darkened the mood. These prophecies hinted at an even greater cosmic conflict, a primordial struggle predating Heaven and Earth. Their ominous warnings, wrapped in symbolism, fueled speculation and fear.

The war with Siberius, it seemed, was only a prelude to darker times.

Azrael, the Great Angel, bore the heaviest burden. From his perch on Heaven's highest spire, he saw not triumph but a wounded realm teetering on the brink. Council meetings devolved into acrimonious debate, archangels jealously guarding their status while veterans demanded recognition. The treasury was depleted, and rebuilding efforts were slowed by material shortages, labor bottlenecks, and disputes over priorities. Azrael was forced to make agonizing choices, aware that every decision left someone disappointed and every compromise risked further division.

The fate of captured demons and fallen angels became a flashpoint. Hardliners, driven by grief and anger, demanded execution, while others pleaded for compassion and rehabilitation. Azrael, torn between principles of justice and mercy, understood that the council's decision would define Heaven's future and its moral character alike.

Resource allocation and the distribution of spoils remained contentious. Lower-ranking angels, the true heroes of the war, demanded equity, while senior figures clung to privilege. Azrael, as mediator, walked a tightrope—every budget, every project, every gesture scrutinized for evidence of bias or favoritism.

The question of sharing advanced technology with Earth added to the turmoil. Some angels saw value in strengthening their allies, others feared their gifts would be misused. The dilemma underscored Heaven's uncertainty about its role: isolation or engagement, self-preservation or cooperation.

The wounds of war reached far beyond Heaven. The trauma reverberated through its alliance with Earth, eroding trust and sparking new doubts about the wisdom of their partnership. The healing centers, overflowing with the broken and traumatized, became symbols of the immense cost of victory. Azrael spent countless hours at these centers, offering comfort where he could, but often feeling the inadequacy of words in the face of so much suffering.

Heaven's hierarchy, once unassailable, was now in crisis. The lower ranks, emboldened by their wartime sacrifices, sought a greater voice. The old guard resisted, fearing chaos and the erosion of order. Azrael, ever patient, tried to bridge the divide, but reconciliation remained elusive. The price of victory was measured not only in ruined citadels but in bitter, unresolved grievances and shifting allegiances.

Siberius' defeat brought little certainty. Rumors of his survival and resurgence spread. Intelligence suggested he was regrouping, seeking new allies among the cosmos' shadowy powers. The threat of his return—or the emergence of an even greater danger—cast a permanent shadow over Heaven's future.

The debate over the fate of the vanquished demons grew more heated. Calls for retribution clashed with arguments for redemption. The outcome remained unsettled, fueling further discord within the council and among the angelic host.

The war had also revealed Heaven's strategic vulnerabilities. The scale of Siberius' rebellion exposed flaws in defense and planning, prompting a sweeping overhaul of security and vigilance. Resource allocation for these reforms competed with the urgent needs of reconstruction.

The repercussions of war rippled outward, unsettling the balance of power across the cosmos. Old alliances were strained, new ones forged. The structure of interdimensional relations became more complicated and precarious. Each decision carried implications far beyond Heaven's borders.

In the midst of rebuilding, Azrael established new healing initiatives: trauma-focused teams, memorial gardens to honor the fallen, and programs to foster community among the wounded. Yet these efforts often felt insufficient against the ocean of grief. The angels' collective spirit, once a source of unity and strength, was now fractured and searching for meaning.

Internal unrest simmered. Demands for reform and representation grew louder, especially from those who had risked the most. The celestial council, divided over mercy or justice for their enemies, embodied Heaven's larger struggle for direction and identity.

Externally, the threat was ever-present. Siberius' escape and the murmurings of new, more dangerous adversaries left little space for complacency. Azrael understood that their peace was fragile—a respite before another storm. Preparation and unity were essential, yet difficult to achieve in the face of so much internal discord.

Technology, once a source of pride, became a matter of concern. The protocols for sharing advancements with Earth were re-examined, weighing the risk of misuse against the need for trust and partnership. Azrael recognized that sustainable peace required more than just military strength; it demanded genuine understanding and cooperation, both within Heaven and in its alliances.

The true price of victory was now clear: not just the loss of lives and splendor, but a relentless commitment to healing, vigilance, and reform. The path forward would be neither easy nor certain. Internal division, external threats, and the scars of trauma presented formidable challenges.

Yet amidst the uncertainty, hope remained. The angels, tempered by adversity, recognized the fragility of their existence and the necessity of unity. The lessons of war—humility, vigilance, and the value of life—would guide their steps. Azrael, bearing the weight of leadership, resolved to safeguard not only Heaven's walls but the spirit of its people.

Their new beginning was not a return to innocence, but a hard-won dawn following a long night. The future was unpredictable, but the resilience of the angels, their hard-earned wisdom, and their shared sense of purpose offered a glimmer of light amidst the lingering shadows. The true battle, Azrael knew, had only just begun.

Chapter 11: Whispers from the Past

Subtle whispers began to drift through Heaven, like the faint rustling of forgotten scrolls in the Grand Archives. These were not mere echoes, but fragments of ancient knowledge—half-remembered prophecies and obscured histories that hinted at conflicts far older and more profound than the current rebellion. As Azrael tirelessly sought to comprehend the full implications of Siberius' uprising, he delved deeper into these forgotten chronicles, uncovering tales not only of past angelic dissent but of primordial forces that had once shaped the destinies of Heaven and Hell alike.

Legacies of Rebellion and Forgotten Wars

One legend told of "The Benevolent One," an angel of immense power who challenged Heaven's rigid order, seeking a more egalitarian celestial society. His movement, less violent and more philosophical than Siberius', spawned the "Harmonists," whose calls for balance and cooperation were ultimately suppressed but left lingering ideals of reform that resonated among Heaven's lower ranks. Their peaceful vision stood in stark contrast to the recent brutalities, suggesting that dissent could be a force for progress as much as for destruction.

Another, darker history surfaced: the War of the Obsidian Shards, a cataclysmic and largely concealed conflict where Heaven battled the "Voidborn," ethereal entities from beyond the known dimensions. These beings sought to consume all creation, and Heaven's desperate resistance culminated in the use of a devastating weapon—the Obsidian Shards—whose residual chaos still haunted the celestial realm. These ancient struggles mirrored the current threats, reinforcing the reality that existential dangers often arose from beyond the familiar order, and that unchecked ambition risked catastrophic consequences.

Azrael's quest also exposed the existence of ancient pacts between archangels and demonic entities—a clandestine alliance forged in pursuit of power, resulting in a tenuous peace built on mutual suspicion and the sharing of forbidden knowledge. These revelations suggested that the present-day alliances and betrayals were not new phenomena but part of a recurring cycle, rooted in the complicated interplay of ambition and necessity.

Prophecies and Artifacts: Warning and Hope

Within a secret and heavily-guarded celestial library, Azrael and a select group of archangels unearthed prophecies inscribed on obsidian tablets and ancient scrolls. These were not straightforward predictions, but cryptic allegories steeped in arcane language and symbolism—difficult to interpret, even by the most learned. The prophecies spoke of several key events:

- The Shattering: A cataclysmic event that would fracture the celestial sphere, preceding an even greater darkness—one not from Hell, but from a reality-defying void.
- The Seven Seals: Mystical barriers imprisoning an entity of unimaginable entropy. Their weakening threatened to unleash chaos, but the prophecies hinted at the possibility of reinforcing them—if only the right conditions could be understood.
- Celestial Convergence: A time when the boundaries between Heaven, Hell, and the mortal realm would blur, creating both opportunities for alliances and risks of betrayal and unchecked power.

Debate raged among the archangels over whether to interpret these prophecies literally, metaphorically, or as warnings meant to guide preparation rather than foretell fate. Azrael himself remained skeptical but recognized the urgent need to learn from the past and to shape destiny through action rather than resignation.

Several relics were referenced within these prophecies—powerful artifacts from ancient wars, each carrying both promise and peril:

- The Scepter of Aethelred: A staff capable of controlling, amplifying, or disrupting celestial energy.
- The Mirror of Souls: A prophetic artifact revealing potential futures, dangerous to the sanity of those who gazed upon it too long.

The search for these artifacts was fraught with peril, as many were protected by guardians, curses, or could potentially unleash even greater calamities if mishandled. Yet, Azrael understood their recovery was vital—not just for their power, but for the knowledge they might yield about the ancient threats now re-emerging.

The Quest for Relics: Trials and Sacrifices

The first tangible clue came as a cryptic message embedded within a fragment of a shattered star, pointing to the "Aegis of the First Dawn"—a shield forged from primordial light. Azrael assembled a team of trusted archangels, including Raphael, Gabriel, and Uriel, to seek the relic. Their perilous journey through the void and a nightmare-haunted cavern tested their resolve and skills. After fierce battles and deciphering ancient runes, they claimed the Aegis, though not without profound cost.

Further whispers pointed to other legendary relics:

- The Sword of Michael: A sun-forged blade capable of defeating the mightiest demons, hidden in a twilight-shrouded world.

- The Helm of Azathoth: A helmet granting reality-altering power but threatening madness, its retrieval requiring forays into unstable dimensions.
- Additional Relics: The Harmonious Orb (balance-restoring), Staff of Thoth (magical conduit), and Lyre of Orpheus (soothing or manipulating emotion)—each presenting unique dangers and requiring a mix of combat, intellect, and willpower to obtain.

Every artifact recovered brought Heaven closer to securing the Seven Seals, but it also revealed the scale of Siberius' ambition. He sought not merely conquest but the unraveling of creation itself, using the scattered artifacts to shatter the Seals and unleash primordial chaos.

Pormis and the Shattering of Certainty

The final, most elusive relic—the Celestial Mirror—led Azrael's team beyond space and time, through realms of shifting energy and impossible geometry. There, in the heart of a fortress guarded by sentient automatons, they encountered a presence more ancient and powerful than any they'd known: Pormis, a primordial entity from the dawn of creation. Pormis revealed that the true struggle was not simply between Heaven and Hell, but between forces seeking to preserve order and those wishing to remake existence.

Pormis offered Azrael the chance to join him in reshaping creation, a seductive but dangerous offer. Azrael refused, choosing loyalty to the values of hope and preservation over the lure of unchecked power. The ensuing battle shook the very foundations of reality, with Azrael wielding the power of the recovered artifacts to repel Pormis—though at terrible cost and with the knowledge that Pormis would return.

The Aftermath: A Precarious Hope

The war's end left Heaven physically and spiritually scarred. The celestial council grappled with internal discord, questions of reform, and the haunting knowledge that Pormis' threat was only delayed. The cosmic balance remained fragile, and the unity of the angelic host was tested as never before. The artifacts, powerful as they were, had only barely averted disaster.

Azrael returned not as a triumphant hero, but as a leader burdened by knowledge and responsibility. The struggle against Siberius and even the primordial entities was not a singular event, but part of an ongoing, cyclical war for the soul of creation—a war that would shape Heaven, Hell, and all realms for ages to come. The fragile peace was merely an interlude; the true battle, as the whispers from the past had always warned, had only just begun.

Chapter 12: New Threats Emerge

The celestial court, once resplendent with the light of a thousand suns, now bore the scars of battle. Shattered pillars and fractured arches carried the legacy of Pormis' destructive power, and the air still vibrated with the echoes of the cataclysm that had shaken Heaven's foundations. Standing upon a battered balcony, Azrael surveyed the ravaged landscape, the victory over Pormis a hollow triumph in an endless war that stretched to the dawn of creation.

Pormis, an ancient force predating the gods themselves, had revealed to Azrael that the struggle was not merely between Heaven and Hell, but woven into the fabric of existence itself—a conflict between the forces that sought to preserve order and those wishing to remake reality. Siberius and his demonic legions were pawns in a larger, more insidious game, their attacks meant to weaken Heaven and prepare it for a far more devastating onslaught.

The whispers of ancient prophecy, once barely noticed, now thundered in Azrael's mind after Pormis' revelations. They spoke of other primordial powers—entities older and mightier than even Pormis—whose slumber had been stirred by the recent war. These beings, true architects of the primordial conflict, awaited their moment to seize control, their motives inscrutable, their very existence blurring the boundary between good and evil.

Azrael's faith in a simple cosmic dichotomy shattered. The universe was revealed to be a tangled web of competing forces, a tapestry woven from both light and shadow. The archangels below, their celestial armor battered and wings drooping, reflected the exhaustion and dread that now gripped Heaven. The threat of Siberius remained, but it had become clear that he was a mere front for the deeper chaos now threatening all realms.

Reports from Earth spoke of demonic activity on an unprecedented scale: the emergence of "super-demons," creatures of raw, ancient malevolence, far beyond the power of any foes the archangels had previously faced. Simultaneously, the awakening of beings long banished—such as Xalzar, the Shadowbinder, and Kena, Mistress of Deceit—signaled that the ancient pacts which kept primordial evils at bay were unraveling. Their return was a certainty, not a possibility.

Heaven's celestial armies were depleted and demoralized after the conflict with Pormis, their ranks thin and morale shaken. Azrael knew that only decisive action could tip the balance. He began to reorganize the celestial legions, retraining angels for unconventional warfare and incorporating the recovered artifacts into their arsenal. Recognizing that Heaven alone could not withstand the coming storm, he sought alliances with other celestial and cosmic entities, forging fragile coalitions with ancient powers that had previously remained neutral.

Meanwhile, whispers of prophecy grew more persistent—of a coming "Great Devourer," a being whose arrival would threaten the annihilation of all existence. Hints that Pormis was merely its harbinger suggested the true enemy still lay ahead, and the stakes had never been higher.

Azrael's leadership was tested as never before. He convened a council of the archangels, laying out an audacious strategy: offensive action against Siberius' forces on Earth, a campaign to seal the rifts threatening to unleash ancient evils, and a desperate attempt to cement alliances with the enigmatic Cosmic Guardians—neutral entities who protected the balance of the universe but had long remained aloof from celestial affairs.

Raphael, renowned for his diplomatic acumen, led the mission to the Guardians, navigating realms of shifting reality and presenting Heaven's case for cosmic intervention. The negotiations were subtle and complex: the Guardians' alliance was not military but strategic, providing knowledge, guidance, and access to ancient artifacts, all of which would come at the cost of maintaining the cosmic balance. Their help was invaluable but fragile, dependent on Heaven's adherence to their principles.

Heaven's alliance with the Guardians changed the tactical landscape. The war was no longer a binary clash; it became a web of shifting alliances and hidden motives. Internal dissent simmered among the archangels—some mistrusted the Guardians' enigmatic ways, while others saw them as essential allies. Azrael walked a diplomatic tightrope, maintaining fragile unity in the face of ideological differences.

On the infernal side, Siberius' authority unraveled. The super-demons, unchecked and hungry for destruction, refused to be controlled. Kena, ever the manipulator, exploited the divisions, whispering promises of power and sowing distrust among the ranks. Xalzar, with blunt force, tried to enforce order but only deepened the chaos. The ancient evils, united only by hatred of Heaven, soon fell into their own rivalries and infighting, fracturing what little remained of their alliance.

Heaven seized this opportunity. Azrael deployed angelic operatives trained in psychological warfare to further exacerbate the divisions among their enemies. These agents spread rumors and misinformation, accelerating the disintegration of the infernal alliance. The conflict evolved from open battle into a war of cunning, manipulation, and secret alliances, with both sides seeking to exploit the weaknesses of the other.

As the war's complexity grew, so did the uncertainty. The lines between good and evil blurred. Victory was contingent not solely on might, but on the ability to navigate a tumultuous landscape of shifting loyalties and enigmatic allies. The celebration of victory in Heaven was subdued, overshadowed by a sense of foreboding and the awareness that peace was, at best, transitory.

The Cosmic Guardians' support remained ambiguous—never direct intervention, but subtle manipulation of fate and access to ancient secrets. Their cryptic pronouncements and long-term strategies frustrated some archangels, especially pragmatic leaders like Raphael, who found their indirectness maddening.

Yet there was no denying their influence, and Heaven's survival depended on maintaining their favor.

The internal struggles of the infernal forces only intensified. Kena's manipulations pitted the super-demons against Siberius, undermined Xalzar's authority, and shattered the fragile unity of the ancient evils. The result was chaos: disorganized attacks, wasted resources, and mounting paranoia. Siberius, once feared, became a weakened figurehead, ignored by his own followers.

Azrael, vigilant and adaptive, continued to exploit these divisions, intensifying psychological operations that further destabilized the enemy while striving to keep Heaven's alliances intact. Yet the situation remained precarious. The alliances with the Guardians demanded strict adherence to the cosmic balance, and any misstep—an act of aggression or moment of hubris—could result in their withdrawal and leave Heaven exposed.

The war had become a struggle not just of armies, but of will, patience, and diplomacy. The lines between friend and foe shifted with every strategic move. The very nature of reality seemed strained, as ancient entities vied for power, alliances formed and dissolved, and the fate of existence hung in the balance.

Amid this uncertainty, Kena's influence spread relentlessly through the ranks of darkness, fanning the flames of ambition, distrust, and betrayal. With every division she sowed, the power of the infernal legions diminished, but so too did the stability of the cosmic order. The cost of victory grew ever higher, threatening to exceed the cost of defeat.

Azrael, bearing the weight of Heaven's future, pressed on. He understood that the battle was not merely for the supremacy of Heaven, but for the survival of all creation. The fragile peace won in the wake of Pormis' defeat was riddled with cracks— internal tensions, suspicious alliances, and the ever-present threat of ancient evils poised to return.

The conflict evolved into a precarious chess game, played on a cosmic scale—a struggle where hope and despair, unity and discord, coexisted in a tenuous equilibrium. The true battle, Azrael knew, had only just begun. The unity of Heaven, the cunning of its enemies, and the fragile cooperation of the Cosmic Guardians would determine the outcome of a war whose consequences would echo across all realms for eternity.

Chapter 13: The Legacy of War

The Scars Upon Heaven, Hell, and Earth

The celestial plains, once radiant with divine light, lay marred and transformed by the cataclysmic war between Heaven and Hell. Apocalyptic clashes had left vast craters, shattered mountains, and scorched landscapes. Rivers of celestial fire, symbols of power and vitality, solidified into obsidian streams that leeched heat and poisoned the land. The air hung thick with the scent of brimstone and the echoes of celestial screams—a haunting reminder that Heaven itself had been irrevocably changed.

The damage extended far beyond physical devastation. Among the angelic legions, pride and unity gave way to trauma and loss. Warriors who once soared confidently now bore tattered wings and haunted gazes, struggling to adapt to a tenuous peace. Nightmares of fallen comrades and infernal horrors plagued their sleep, and faith in divine order wavered. The healing process was slow and fraught, as psychological wounds ran deeper than any visible scar.

Heaven's societal structure was equally disrupted. The rigid hierarchy, once unchallenged, faced scrutiny from the younger generation—angels who had grown up amid war and now demanded reform. At odds with the elders who clung to tradition, these voices of dissent exposed generational divides, threatening further internal conflict. Antiquated laws and customs proved inadequate for the challenges of post-war life, and the very concept of celestial justice was questioned.

For its leaders, the war's toll was profound. Azrael, architect of victory, bore the burden of countless losses, his resolve frayed by the weight of command and the cost of survival. The faces of fallen angels haunted him, each sacrifice a heavy reminder of the price paid. Raphael, pragmatic and direct, found his strategies tested by the enigmatic Cosmic Guardians. Forced to accept the limits of brute force, he learned the value of patience and indirect influence, gaining a grudging respect for their cryptic methods.

Within the ranks of archangels, unity dissolved into shifting alliances and suspicion. Some embraced the reforms advocated by younger angels, while others resisted, driven by fear and nostalgia for the old order. The resulting atmosphere of distrust threatened to unravel the fragile peace.

On the infernal side, the aftermath was equally chaotic and destructive. Siberius' authority lay in ruins, as super-demons turned on each other and ancient evils succumbed to self-destructive rivalries. Kena exploited these divisions with cunning manipulation, consolidating her own power. Xalzar, once a feared enforcer, found himself marginalized, unable to unite the fractured forces of darkness. The infernal legions splintered, vulnerable to both internal collapse and external exploitation.

Earth bore its own scars. Celestial energies unleashed during the war triggered earthquakes, volcanic eruptions, and environmental devastation. Skies darkened with ash, rivers became toxic, and fertile lands turned barren. The planet's ecosystems reeled, struggling to recover from the apocalyptic onslaught.

Societal repercussions were severe. Human civilizations, caught in the crossfire, saw great cities reduced to rubble and entire populations wiped out. Survivors grappled with trauma, loss, and a shattered sense of faith. The war left a deep mark on humanity's collective consciousness—a pervasive fear of the unknown and a profound sense of vulnerability. Faith in institutions eroded, creating a power vacuum quickly filled by opportunistic leaders and cults, leading to social and political instability.

The long-term consequences of the war extended far beyond the immediate devastation. Environmental damage persisted for centuries, rendering many regions uninhabitable and fueling ongoing instability. Societal disruption led to new forms of tyranny and oppression, and psychological scars lingered in the minds of survivors. The war's legacy was one of loss and transformation—a deceptive peace overlaying deep-seated divisions and unresolved conflict.

The Generational Impact

Children born in the aftermath inherited a world irrevocably altered by trauma. In Heaven, playgrounds became reminders of battlefields, and celestial games echoed the stories of war whispered by grieving parents. Their lullabies were mournful hymns, and the vibrant hues of their wings were dulled by the pervasive sense of loss. Many angelic children bore physical anomalies—twisted wings, missing limbs—manifestations of lingering cosmic wounds. Medical facilities struggled to provide care amid limited resources, and families faced a lifetime of challenges.

On Earth, generational trauma was equally pervasive. Communities decimated by war left children growing up amidst ruins, their stories filled with loss and suffering. Parents, burdened by PTSD and survivor's guilt, struggled to provide stability, trapping families in cycles of poverty and emotional distress. High rates of anxiety, depression, and PTSD plagued entire generations, shattering trust and leaving many children with behavioral problems and a profound sense of insecurity.

The ripple effects of trauma reshaped societies, eroding faith in institutions and fostering cynicism. Relationships suffered— parents and children struggled to connect, marriages crumbled, and communities fractured. The lack of emotional support perpetuated mental health crises, and social dysfunction became widespread.

Heaven's hierarchy, already strained, faced further erosion as younger angels demanded a more just and equitable society. Generational divides widened, threatening another era of conflict. On Earth, the breakdown of social structures fueled crime, unrest, and the rise of authoritarian leaders who exploited chaos for power.

The legacy of war seeped into every aspect of society. Institutions meant to provide stability were overwhelmed, and the magnitude of trauma challenged the very foundations of celestial and human realms. The memory of conflict became a haunting presence, shaping destinies and clouding the future with uncertainty.

Rebuilding and Transformation

In Heaven, reconstruction was monumental but incomplete. The celestial city, restored in form, lacked its former spirit. The laughter of angels was subdued, and sacred places felt hollow. The Great Angel oversaw the rebuilding, burdened by loss and the emotional scars of survivors.

Politically, Heaven's old guard clashed with reformers. The establishment of a new council—more inclusive and representative—met resistance and sparked debates over justice, authority, and the relationship with Earth. The transition was fraught, and old wounds made peace elusive.

Earth's recovery was even more daunting. Cities lay in ruins, economies crippled, and ecosystems devastated. Psychological trauma persisted, with survivors struggling to adapt. Cooperation between nations was essential, but disparities in resources and power led to tension and conflict. Some nations sought to exploit chaos, while others faced famine and hardship.

Technological innovation became a beacon of hope. The war's destruction inspired advances in defense, construction, and environmental restoration. Celestial energies were harnessed for peaceful purposes, powering cities and agriculture. New agricultural technologies helped mitigate food shortages, and scientific progress offered tools for rebuilding.

The cultural landscape shifted dramatically. The war spurred reassessment of religious beliefs, moral values, and humanity's place in the cosmos. Artists and writers grappled with themes of loss and resilience, creating new narratives that reflected a changed world. The trauma of war fostered cooperation and a global support network for mental health.

Despite hardship, hope emerged. Shared suffering forged new alliances and a deeper sense of interconnectedness. Movements advocating for social justice and environmental protection gained momentum. International cooperation grew, though challenges remained—threats of renewed conflict, economic inequality, and persistent environmental damage.

Enduring Consequences and the Dawn of a New Era

The new world order was marked by vulnerability, uncertainty, and a relentless drive to rebuild. Nations forged alliances for protection, and the specter of celestial invasion prompted global efforts to bolster defenses. Economic recovery was slow, and social divisions persisted.

Cultural and religious beliefs were reshaped, challenging old narratives and inspiring new forms of expression. The environment suffered lasting damage, with mutations in plants and animals and destabilized climate patterns. International cooperation was critical but often hampered by distrust and limited resources.

The psychological scars of war remained pervasive, with mental health crises straining support systems. The generational impact extended far beyond those who witnessed the conflict, shaping societal development and perpetuating trauma. The dust of war had settled, but the scars lingered—a constant reminder of the price paid and the challenges ahead.

In Heaven, rebuilding efforts continued, guided by a new council determined to foster unity and reform. The old hierarchy was challenged, and debates raged over the future direction of celestial society. The Great Angel promoted diplomacy and inclusivity, though skepticism and fear of renewed conflict persisted.

On Earth, cooperation and conflict coexisted. Technological advances aided recovery, but disparities in resources led to ongoing tension. The cultural response was marked by resilience—a search for meaning, hope, and solidarity in the face of adversity.

From the ashes of destruction, a new era began to rise. The experience of war fostered global unity and a drive for justice. Movements for social equality and environmental stewardship gained strength, and international alliances solidified. Yet the threat of renewed cosmic conflict loomed, and the task of rebuilding—physically, emotionally, and politically—remained immense.

The legacy of the celestial war was complex: devastation and transformation, loss and resilience. Heaven, Hell, and Earth were forever altered, their scars a testament to the enduring consequences of cosmic conflict. The fragile peace was both an achievement and a warning, reminding all realms of the need for vigilance, cooperation, and hope as they faced an uncertain future.

Chapter 14: Shadows of the Future

The Gathering Storm After the Celestial War

The fragile peace that followed the cataclysmic war between Heaven and Hell proved to be a brief respite, a pause before the emergence of a new, insidious threat. Beneath the surface of celestial recovery, whispers of unrest flowed through Heaven— not from the remnants of Siberius' rebellion, but from beings that defied all known dichotomies. Known as the Undyn, these entities were pure shadow, older than the cosmos itself, feeding on discord and chaos. Their influence seeped into both Heaven and Earth, spreading doubt, mistrust, and division.

The Rise of the Undyn

The Undyn operated in secrecy, veiled in impenetrable darkness, subtly manipulating emotions and perceptions. Their origins and ultimate goals remained a mystery: some speculated they sought eternal night and chaos, while others believed them to be agents of an ancient cosmic force whose intentions remained unfathomable.

Minor incidents in Heaven—skirmishes between angelic legions, rumors of betrayal—signaled the Undyn's growing influence. The recently formed council, tasked with guiding Heaven's recovery, found itself paralyzed by internal division. Old wounds reopened, and trust eroded, threatening to undo the hard-won peace.

On Earth, the aftermath of the celestial war left humanity vulnerable. Extremist and nationalist movements surged, fueled by fear and uncertainty, their ideologies warped by the Undyn's subtle manipulations. Alliances frayed as mistrust grew, and the global effort to rebuild faltered under escalating political and social tensions.

Sabotage and Discord

Even scientific progress was affected. Research into harnessing celestial energies faced inexplicable setbacks—accidents, sabotage, and anomalies plagued the hopeful projects. The healing of mental and emotional wounds stalled, as support systems and therapists themselves became divided and suspicious. Across both realms, the Undyn's whispers undermined recovery, sowing seeds of discord that fractured communities and institutions.

Reality itself began to show signs of strain. Temporal distortions, gravitational anomalies, and surges in celestial energy occurred worldwide, at first imperceptibly but then with increasing frequency and intensity. The very fabric of existence seemed threatened.

The Challenge of Unity

Both Heaven and Earth now faced a new enemy, more elusive and dangerous than Siberius and his demonic legions. Old divisions and lingering trauma made unity difficult. The Great Angel, burdened with the task of rallying celestial forces, struggled against resistance from the old guard and skepticism about the new generation of leaders. Voices of dissent, amplified by the Undyn, threatened to tear Heaven apart.

Earth's situation was equally dire. Nations, battered by war and economic hardship, found it hard to maintain unity. The Undyn exploited every weakness, driving wedges between allies and pushing humanity closer to chaos. The alliances forged in the crucible of war began to crumble, undermined by fear and suspicion.

Yet hope persisted. A small group of angels recognized that the Undyn thrived on division and fear. They began a quiet campaign to unite Heaven and Earth, believing only cooperation could defeat this new enemy. The path was perilous, but determination grew among those who saw the stakes—survival of all creation.

Political Intrigue in Heaven and Earth

Within Heaven, the formation of the unified council became its own battleground. Archangel Azrael, representing the old guard, pushed for a return to traditional hierarchies, arguing that strong, centralized authority was needed to prevent further chaos. Raphael, the progressive strategist admired for his role in the war, advocated for a diverse council that included younger angels and human-angel liaison groups, insisting that collaboration was vital for lasting peace. The ideological clash intensified, with the Undyn exploiting and amplifying every division.

Council meetings devolved into storms of accusation. Azrael's supporters accused Raphael of plotting a power grab, while Raphael's allies countered that Azrael's rigidity endangered Heaven's future. The Great Angel struggled to mediate, his efforts continually undermined by the Undyn.

Beyond the high councils, rivalries between angelic legions reignited. Small disputes, manipulated by the Undyn, escalated into violent clashes. Unity among the angels faded as internal conflict consumed their energy.

On Earth, political instability mirrored the chaos in Heaven. The global community fractured as nationalism and extremism surged, fueled by the Undyn's manipulations. Recovery efforts stalled, resources became scarce, and international agreements collapsed. Even attempts to heal psychological trauma became mired in division and distrust.

The Web of Alliance and Betrayal

As the old alliances in Heaven and Earth broke down, new ones formed—unstable, opportunistic coalitions forged in desperation. Azrael allied with lesser angelic orders, seeking to bolster his strength. Raphael, vulnerable in his idealism, allied with progressive factions and human liaisons, but faced accusations of weakness and betrayal. The Undyn manipulated every side, creating secret pacts and seeding suspicion even among supposed allies.

On Earth, fringe religious groups and corporate interests formed alliances, driven by apocalyptic fervor and the Undyn's subtle influence. These unlikely partnerships posed unpredictable threats to global stability, their actions driven by greed and a thirst for power.

Meanwhile, a new celestial faction emerged—the Silent Watchers. Disillusioned with both main camps in Heaven, they sought to subvert the system from within, forming covert alliances with the Undyn and undermining any attempts at reform or unity. Their motivations, shrouded in secrecy, made them a dangerous wildcard in the growing chaos.

The Great Angel watched as the peace unraveled, his attempts at mediation consistently thwarted by betrayal. The threat of a second, even more devastating war loomed, one not just between Heaven and Hell, but within the very fabric of creation. The game of alliances had reached a critical point; any misstep could mean catastrophe.

Ancient Prophecies and Forgotten Wars

Amidst the turmoil, whispers of forgotten prophecies and ancient texts resurfaced. Archangel Michael, gripped by unease, delved into celestial archives and legends that spoke of an ancient war predating even Heaven and Hell—a primordial conflict whose echoes shaped all of existence.

Fragments of knowledge hinted at a cataclysm known as the "Fracturing," a cosmic explosion resulting from a battle between incomprehensibly powerful entities. Lost civilizations, long gone before humanity, had glimpsed the true nature of this ancient war, leaving behind enigmatic ruins and cryptic texts.

Michael's research suggested that the Undyn was not merely a malevolent force, but a manifestation of the chaotic energy left behind by the Fracturing. Its ultimate goal remained obscured, but clues pointed to its desperate search for ancient artifacts— relics of unimaginable power capable of altering the very fabric of reality. The Undyn's quest for these artifacts raised alarming possibilities: could they end the current conflict, or unleash an even greater catastrophe?

A Cosmic Game and Looming Cataclysm

Deeper investigation connected the ancient war with current events, suggesting that key figures like Siberius echoed names and roles from primordial legends. A cosmic cycle of conflict seemed to repeat across millennia, possibly orchestrated by unseen forces.

The ancient texts spoke of a future cataclysm, an apocalypse even more destructive than the Fracturing, linked to the artifacts and the Undyn's relentless pursuit. Michael theorized that the recent war was but a prelude—a distraction masking a grander conspiracy with stakes far greater than anyone realized.

The burden of this revelation weighed heavily on Michael. He faced existential questions about the nature of good and evil, free will, and destiny, as the cosmology revealed itself to be far more complex and terrifying. The celestial war was only a ripple in a cosmic ocean of struggles, its consequence reaching far beyond immediate concerns.

The ancient mysteries offered hints of a way to break the cycle: the acquisition and proper use of the scattered artifacts. Yet, the texts warned that this path was perilous, requiring courage, sacrifice, and mastery of celestial energies. A single misstep could mean the end of all creation.

Determination Amid Darkness

Michael resolved that the cycle of destruction must end. He would gather allies, harness every resource, and prepare for the ultimate confrontation—a battle that would determine not only the fate of Heaven and Hell, but the survival of existence itself. The threat of cosmic annihilation was immense, but so was his determination to fight for the future.

The celestial gardens now stood as silent witnesses to both tragedy and hope. The revelations of the ancient texts shattered all illusions of safety and certainty, forcing Michael—and indeed all of creation—to confront the chilling reality that the current peace was but a fleeting interlude before a storm of unimaginable proportions.

The ancient prophecies spoke of a cosmic ballet, an endless cycle of creation and destruction. Each conflict, including the recent war, was a step toward an ultimate reckoning. The path to salvation lay shrouded in sacrifice and peril, requiring the courage to face the unknown and the wisdom to break the eternal cycle.

Archangel Michael, battered but resolute, stood among the ruins, determined to face whatever darkness the future held. The next chapter would demand more than strength; it would demand faith, unity, and the willingness to confront the deepest mysteries of existence. The fight for survival, for the very soul of creation, had begun—and the outcome would define all that was, is, and would ever be.

Chapter 15: Epilogue

The celestial gardens lay still, their serenity broken only by the sigh of the wind amid shattered blossoms and scarred arches. Michael stood among the ruins, the aftermath of Heaven and Hell's cataclysmic war pressing upon him like a weight beyond mortal measure. Victory, if it could be called that, felt bitter and incomplete. The price was steep: countless angels lost, their songs silenced, their light extinguished. Heaven itself, once gleaming with divine perfection, now bore deep scars—a testament to the ferocity of Siberius' rebellion and the demonic legions' dreadful power.

Faces, memories, and losses haunted Michael. Raphael, Gabriel, Uriel—names that echoed through his soul. Their sacrifices became guiding stars, but their absence left unspeakable voids. Raphael's courage, Gabriel's loyalty, and Uriel's wisdom had shaped the fight, yet their deaths underscored the vulnerability of even Heaven's greatest. The echoes of their final cries lingered, a constant reminder of mortality within immortality.

The war was a brutal clash of celestial fire and demonic fury. Siberius' blade had left Michael both physically and emotionally scarred. Siberius' power, Michael realized, was not solely his own—it was channeled from a dark, ancient force, the Undyn, whose influence manipulated the course of events. Heaven's defenders had been pawns in a cosmic game, the true scale of which was unfathomable. What seemed a struggle between good and evil was revealed as a ripple in a wider, more ominous cosmic ocean.

After the war, Heaven's reconstruction began—painful, slow, and steeped in grief. The gardens were reduced to wastelands, celestial melodies replaced by quiet laments. Yet, a fragile hope flickered amid the devastation. The angelic host, though battered, remained resilient; their faith, tested to the brink, did not break. Instead, it acquired new depth—a wisdom born of suffering, a resolve tempered by adversity. The lessons of war were harsh: complacency, once fostered by trust in divine order, was shattered. Ancient prophecies, previously dismissed as legend, now loomed threateningly, suggesting a cosmic cycle of conflict, orchestrated by forces neither angel nor demon could fully comprehend.

The revelation of the Undyn's manipulation was perhaps the most chilling. The war had been but a diversion, masking a deeper, grander conspiracy. The angels, once confident in their purpose and power, now understood their place as pieces in a game played by primordial entities. The vaunted invincibility of Heaven was exposed as illusion; their reality, fractured and vulnerable.

Still, the spirit of the angels endured. Their loyalty to God and to each other became their shield against despair. They fought bravely, united by the memory of the fallen and fueled by the hope that their struggle was not in vain. The scars left by the war—architectural, emotional, philosophical—served as reminders of both loss and strength.

Michael's burden grew. As leader, he bore responsibility for healing, rebuilding, and guiding Heaven's survivors. Mending wounds, comforting the bereaved, and restoring faith—these were monumental tasks, requiring every ounce of wisdom and resolve. The war had not only destroyed bodies but had shaken the very foundations of angelic faith. Doubt crept in, whispering questions about divine justice, God's plan, and the meaning of existence. The certainty that had governed their world was now replaced by vulnerability and contemplation.

The emotional toll ran deep. Memories of the fallen haunted every moment. The labor of rebuilding was itself a metaphor for healing—a painstaking process symbolic of the resilience required to move forward. The once vibrant celestial nurseries, now subdued, echoed the somber mood. Fewer cherubs were born, their cries fragile against a backdrop of loss. Yet, life persisted, and new generations of angels emerged, shaped by the aftermath of conflict.

The New Generation: Kena and Azrael

Among this new generation, Kena and Azrael stood as symbols of Heaven's altered future. Kena, introspective and empathetic, carried wisdom beyond her years, her heart attuned to the sorrows of the celestial realm. Azrael, the son of a fallen warrior, was fiery and driven—his life's purpose shaped by the desire to avenge his father and prevent further loss.

Their friendship reflected Heaven's duality: Kena embodied hope and healing; Azrael, anger and the will for justice. Their contrasting personalities, yet shared journey, demonstrated the complexity of the postwar celestial order. They were united by the stories of heroism and sacrifice, raised on tales that were honest about both victory and tragedy.

The new generation did not inherit a simple vision of good versus evil. Instead, they understood nuance—demons who fought from desperation rather than pure malice, angels who struggled with doubt. Their worldview was shaped by tragedy and resilience, by the monuments and scars that remained. The physical and emotional reminders of the war served as living testaments to the struggle, guiding the new angels as they sought to rebuild a better Heaven.

Questions and Challenges

The end of the war did not mean the end of uncertainty. The threat of super-demons, powerful unknown entities, hovered over Heaven. The celestial hierarchy, shattered by loss, was in flux, with new leaders and factions vying for influence. The political landscape was fraught with rivalries and the potential for further strife, making the work of rebuilding not only physical but profoundly political and philosophical.

Faith itself was under siege. The war's devastation had forced even the most devout to question the nature of God's plan. Was the Great Angel's intervention a stroke of luck or an element of a larger scheme? The absence of clear divine answers led to speculation, skepticism, and a reassessment of long-held beliefs. These existential questions—about justice, suffering, and the cosmic order—became central to Heaven's reconstruction.

The act of rebuilding was loaded with symbolic meaning. Every architectural choice, every new garden, every nursery became a reflection of the angels' internal debates about identity and destiny. Kena and Azrael, carrying the weight of both hope and grief, exemplified this struggle. Their journey was not only about restoring Heaven's walls but about redefining purpose and faith in the wake of immense loss.

The Road Ahead

The defeat of Siberius brought only a brief reprieve. The super-demons persisted as a shadowy threat, and the doubts sown by war lingered. Political factions jockeyed for power, and the philosophical questions posed by suffering and evil remained unresolved. Kena and Azrael, along with their generation, faced the daunting challenge of not only rebuilding Heaven but also healing the spiritual and existential wounds left by conflict.

Their friendship and determination stood as beacons in the darkness. Through pragmatic preparation and empathetic reflection, they sought to make sense of the new world. They compiled knowledge, rebuilt alliances, and tried to foster unity. Yet, the future was unwritten, fraught with peril, and shaped by the legacy of loss.

Legacy and Hope

The celestial winds whispered tales of prophecy, alliance, and betrayal. The stars themselves seemed to await the next chapter in the cosmic drama. The rebuilding of Heaven was more than restoring structures—it was about reaffirming identity, nurturing hope, and embracing the complexity of faith. The new generation was tasked with forging a future not defined by the darkness of the past, but by the possibility of renewal.

The epilogue's final image was one of quiet contemplation—a solemn understanding that the journey was just beginning. Heaven's survivors, shaped by war and loss, faced the unknown with resolve. The unanswered questions, the lingering uncertainties, defined not an ending, but a prelude. The next chapter awaited, its tapestry woven from the threads of sacrifice, resilience, and the enduring hope for a future free from the shadows of conflict.